KU-198-999

Cat and Mouse on the farm

Ray Gibson

Reading consultant: Karen Bryant-Mole

Illustrated by Graham Round

Designed by Amanda Barlow

Edited by Robyn Gee and Jenny Tyler

Parent's notes

This book is for you and your child to use together. It is aimed at children aged three and up who are just ready to learn to read their first words. It contains early reading activities which will help bridge the gap between prereading activities and first solo storybooks.

The main purpose of the book is to build your child's confidence and give a positive attitude to reading. It does not follow one particular method of teaching reading, but takes a varied approach which will not conflict with anything your child is learning at school.

On some pages there is just a simple story for you to read to your child. Being read to is a very important part of the process of learning to read. Feeling that books are a source of pleasure provides children with a strong incentive to read by themselves. It also helps to improve their listening and concentration skills and to develop their sense of what a story is.

There are instructions on each page to tell you what to do and footnotes to explain how the activity is contributing to your child's reading skills. The words in blue are for your child to read. Point them out and help your child to guess what they say.

The book builds towards a simple story for your child to read alone. The words used in the story are all introduced and used earlier in the book.

When tackling any of the activities in this book go at your child's natural pace and give plenty of praise and encouragement. It is very important that your reading sessions are enjoyable.

How do you know if your child is ready to read?

There is no definite way of knowing the answer to this. There are, however, some questions you could ask yourself to help you decide.

- Does your child like books?
- Does your child sometimes look at them alone?
- Does your child sometimes pretend she is reading?
- Does your child show an interest when you point out words, or write things down?
- Can your child recognize her own name?

- Does your child know a few letter sounds?
- Does your child ask you what words say?
- Does your child sometimes join in when you read stories she knows well?
- Can your child retell a simple story in the right sequence?

If your answer to most of these questions is "yes", then your child is probably ready to read.

Meet Cat and Mouse

This is Cat. This is Mouse. They live together in this house.

Who is tall? Who is small? Who is hiding in the hall?

Whose boots are blue? Whose boots are red? Who is hiding in this bed?

Their car is parked outside their house. Who will drive it, Cat or Mouse?

Children naturally enjoy rhythm and rhyme and research has shown that this helps them with the process of learning to read.

3

A letter arrives

One morning Cat and Mouse get a letter.

"It's from Farmer Frog!" says Mouse.
"He says we can go and stay on his farm."

Cat is so excited, he can't stand still.

"I can drive the tractor. I can collect the eggs. I can feed the pigs and ride the horses!" he chants as he dances around the room.

"Let's pack," says Mouse.
" We can go today."

Can you see what Cat and Mouse are going to take with them? Is Cat choosing sensible things to take to a farm?

To Cat
and Mouse

Dear Cat and Mouse,

Please come and stay on my farm.

love from Farmer Frog

Reading aloud to children helps to expand their vocabulary and improve their concentration.

Cat and Mouse's journey

They put the bags in their little yellow car and hop in. Mouse drives through the town, past the houses to the leafy country lanes.

"Are we going the right way?" says Cat.

Can you see which way Cat and Mouse must go to reach Farmer Frog's Farm?

To Farmer Frog's Farm

Solving visual puzzles helps develop children's observation, which is vital for learning to distinguish one word from another.

5

Animal words

cow

penguin

tiger

goat

horse

elephant

hen

zebra

sheep

pig

horse
goat
sheep
hen
pig

Before they left home, Cat and Mouse found a book about animals. Can you look at the word underneath each picture and then help Cat and Mouse by saying the word for each animal?

Mouse has made a list of animals they might find on the farm. See if you can match the words on Mouse's list with the words under the pictures.

Spotting pairs of matching words helps children to recognize and remember the shapes made by words.

Arriving on the farm

At last they see a sign.

"To Farmer Frog's Farm,"
reads Mouse.
"It's down here."

As they drive into
the farmyard, they
hear the animals,

"Mooooooo!"

"Baaaaaa!"

"Quaaaack!"

"Hmm," says Mouse.
"I thought farms were nice, quiet places."

Farmer Frog hurries out to meet them.

"You're just in time for supper," he says.
"There's milk from the dairy, fresh bread made with our own wheat and
runny honey from our very own bees."

After supper, Cat wants to take
some pictures with his camera,
but it is too dark. Soon Mouse
is in bed, snoring, but Cat is
still too excited to sleep.

"Tomorrow," he thinks,
"I can be a real farmer."

I spy on the farm

Next morning, Farmer Frog takes Cat and Mouse up High Hill to show them his farm. It is a long, hot climb and they are glad to sit and rest and look through their binoculars.

"What can you see?" asks Farmer Frog.

This game will help your child gain practice with letter sounds. Point out or write down the letters you choose to help your child associate the sound with the correct symbol.

"I spy with my little eye, something beginning with 'puh' ", says Mouse. Cat and Farmer Frog have to guess what it is. Cat guesses "pig" and he is right. It is his turn to choose a letter next. You can play this game too. Pretend you are Cat and Mouse. Take turns to choose something in the picture and say what letter sound it begins with. The other person tries to guess the word.

When children start to read, being able to sound out the first letter of a word is a powerful clue to what the word might be.

Cat takes some photographs

That afternoon Cat and Mouse go out to take some photographs.
These pictures tell the story of what happens to them.

The purpose of this picture story is to encourage children to focus on what is happening in each picture and to translate this into words which build into a story.

Can you tell the story out loud?
Who is angry with Cat and Mouse? Why is he angry?

This skill will be useful when your child comes to stories with words. Clues from the pictures give children the confidence to try the words underneath.

11

Butter the goat

Read this story to your child, pausing when you come to a picture. Let your child say the word for the picture and then carry on reading. Follow the lines with your finger as you read.

A farmer's life is very busy and today [frog] is in a hurry. He has to take some [carrots] to market in the farm [truck] and needs some help on the farm while he is gone.

Mouse is to collect the new-laid [eggs] from the [hen] and Cat is to take Butter, the [goat] to find a fresh patch of [grass] to eat.

"Why is his name "Butter"?" asks [cat] .

"He is not yellow like butter, he is white."

"You will find out," says [frog] .

Butter is tied to the farm [gate] with a big thick [rope] .

"This will be easy," thinks [cat] .

[cat] is wrong.

The minute he has untied the [rope] , Butter the [goat] gives it a very hard tug and pulls it out of Cat's . Then he puts down his head, butts the [gate] open with his [horns] , and trots into the farmyard.

There he begins to chew at a line of [washing] which is hanging out to dry. [Cat] chases after him, but by the time he arrives, Butter the [goat] has chewed up a pair of [trousers], a [shirt] and three [socks].

Then, with [cat] huffing and puffing behind him, Butter the [goat] butts the pile of [boxes] full of [carrots], that [frog] is loading into the [truck].

They all topple over into the [mud].

"Humph! There's no time to wash the [carrots] for market," [frog] says.

[Cat] ties Butter up again.

"All that running has made me hungry," says [cat]. "What is for lunch?"

" [carrot] soup, followed by [carrot] pie with [carrot] cake for dessert", says [frog].

13

Catch the pigs

Feeling a bit fed up with carrots, Cat and Mouse are helping Farmer Frog get the animals back to their places.

It is Cat and Mouse's job to catch the hens, the cows and the pigs. The pigs are the most difficult of all.

Play this game to find out who catches the most pigs - Cat or Mouse.

How to play

One person is Cat, the other person is Mouse. Each person has ten paper counters and a button (make sure they are different). Cat and Mouse take turns rolling the dice, and move their buttons the number of places shown on the dice. If the button lands on an "animal" space, the player has caught that animal and places a

This game will help your child recognize and remember the four words: pig, hen, cow, mud.

counter on the pig-pen, cow field or hen house. If the button lands on a "mud" space, the player stays where she is and the other player puts a pig in the pig-pen. When someone has thrown the right number to land on the finish, count up the counters in the pig-pen to see who is the winner.

Farmer Cat

Read this story to your child, following the lines with your finger. When you get to the words in blue type, stop and encourage your child to try reading them.

Farmer Frog has to go out for the day.
"Who can look after the farm for me?" he says.

"I can!" says Cat. "I can be the farmer. Mouse can help me."

"Who can scrub out the milk churns?" asks Farmer Frog.

"I can. I can,"
says Cat, hopping on one leg.

"Who can fetch the corn and feed the hens?" asks Farmer Frog.

"I can. I can,"
says Cat, jumping up and down.

"Who can collect the apples the wind has blown down?" asks Farmer Frog.

"I can. I can. I can,"
says Cat. "Leave everything to me."

Cat and Mouse wave as Farmer Frog drives off down the lane. Then Cat runs and puts on Farmer Frog's old coat and hat. "I'm a real farmer," he beams and strides off into the farmyard.

Mouse clears up the breakfast things and tidies up the farmhouse. At 11 o'clock he calls Cat for coffee, but Cat is nowhere to be seen. Where is Cat?

Cat is stuck.

Your child will soon begin to recognize the repeating words and will have a sense of achievement from helping you read the story.

He put his head inside a milk churn and he can't get it out.
Mouse rubs some butter on and Cat's head slips out.

"Never mind," says Mouse. "Come and drink
your coffee. I will wash out the churns."

At one o'clock, Mouse makes lunch and calls
Cat again, but Cat is nowhere to be seen.
Where is Cat?

Cat is stuck.

Instead of feeding the hens, he is riding a horse, pretending to be a
cowboy. His tail is caught on a giant thistle. Mouse cuts the thistle down.

"Never mind," says Mouse. "Come and
have some lunch . I will feed the hens."

At six o'clock, Mouse calls Cat for
supper, but Cat is nowhere to be seen.
Where is Cat?

Cat is stuck

He is climbing the apple tree instead of picking up the apples. His coat is
caught on a branch. Mouse gets a ladder.

"Never mind," says Mouse. "Come and have
your supper. I will collect the apples."

After supper, Farmer Frog comes back. He has a
baby piglet. "Who can look after my piglet?" he asks.
Cat stays very quiet.

"I can,"
says Mouse.

The rainy day

Big storm clouds are gathering over Farmer Frog's farm. It is starting to rain. Who, or what, is getting wet?

Are the horses out in the rain or in the stable?

Look at all the pictures to find out which things are in and which are out, then play the game.

in

in

out

Mouse   in

out

To play the game, you need three small pieces of white cardboard. Leave one blank, write "in" on one and "out" on the other. Put all three cards in a bag. You also need five counters, coins or buttons for each player.

One of you has the "Mouse" page, the other has the "Cat" page. Take turns taking a card from the bag. If it

in

out

out

out

in

Cat

says "out", put a counter on an "out" picture on your page. If it says "in", put a counter on an "in" picture on your page. If it is blank, miss a turn.

After each turn, put the card back in the bag and shake it up ready for the next turn.

The winner is the first one to cover all the pictures.

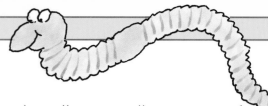

Looking for worms

The words on this page are for you to read. The words on the opposite page are for your child. Start by reading the paragraph below. Then encourage your child to try the words under the picture opposite. Take turns to complete the story.

When the rain stops the hen comes out in the sunshine to look for worms. She scratches and scratches in the earth with her sharp claws, and soon finds a nice fat worm near the apple tree. She pulls at it with her beak.

When Mouse comes along to collect some eggs, he sees the hen pulling and pulling as hard as she can.

"You look as if you need some help," says Mouse.
He opens the gate and comes in to help.

"Hold on tight," says the hen.

Just then, Cat comes skipping up with potato peelings for the pigs. He sees Mouse and the hen, still pulling at the worm.

" I'll pull too," says Cat. " I 'm very strong. Just look at my muscles!"
Cat pulls Mouse, who pulls the hen, who is still pulling the worm.

When Farmer Frog sees them all pulling, he laughs.

"That's not a worm you are pulling," he says. "That is a root. It belongs to the apple tree."

Cat and Mouse stop pulling and start to laugh with Farmer Frog. The hen stops pulling too and sets off to look for a real worm.

In this shared reading activity, your child is given a simplified version of the adult text to read. Give as much help and encouragement as you think is needed.

The hen pulls.

The hen pulls. Mouse pulls.

The hen pulls. Mouse pulls. Cat pulls.

The hen pulls. Mouse pulls. Cat pulls. Farmer Frog laughs.

Stuck in the mud

Cat is in the mud.

Cat is stuck.

The hen pulls Cat.

The cow pulls Cat.

This is a big step for your child. Read the story aloud first if you like, then give lots of encouragement by suggesting your child looks carefully at the pictures and giving first letter sounds as clues.

The pig pulls Cat.

Can Mouse pull Cat out?

Mouse can pull Cat out.

Cat is out.

All the words in this story have been introduced earlier in the book. Repeat some of the earlier pages if you feel your child is not ready for this stage yet.

Goodbye to the farm

When you have read the words below, encourage your child to attempt the words in Cat and Mouse's book.

It is time for Cat and Mouse to go home. Farmer Frog and all the animals come to say goodbye. Cat and Mouse are feeling very sad.

"Never mind," says Cat. "We will have lots of photographs to remind us of the farm."

They collect their photographs from the shop as soon as they can. You can see some of them below.

Can you read what Cat and Mouse have written?

The pig and Mouse

Cat and the hen

Cat and the cow

Farmer Frog and the goat

This page gives your child more opportunities to try reading, building on the confidence acquired on the previous pages.